A Christmas Pudding

Created, Compiled
and Adapted by

David Birney

SAMUEL FRENCH

FOUNDED 1830

New York Hollywood London Toronto

SAMUELFRENCH.COM

ISBN 978-0-573-65125-0   Printed in U.S.A.   #6280

IMPORTANT BILLING AND CREDIT
REQUIREMENTS

To my children, Mollie and Peter and Kate, whose letters to Santa Claus and Christmas hearts began all of this long ago.

To Michele Roberge with gratitude for the gift of her work on this, and her ongoing grace and great heart.

And to the community of Westwood Presbyterian Church and Charles and Claire Orr who have lovingly set the table for The Pudding these many Christmases.

"Christmas—The hush, the star, the baby...people being kind again."

—Elizabeth Jennings

AUTHOR'S NOTES

A Christmas Pudding began as a benefit for the homeless in Los Angeles in 1995, featuring a cast of six actors and a musical consort, a small chorus of some 10 to 12 singers, performing *a cappella* or with the accompaniment of the organ or piano. It has been performed successfully at a small, (500 seat) grey stone neo-Gothic church, the Westwood Presbyterian Church, where it was warmly embraced and has continued since. Following its premiere, it has played, as well, in a variety of locations-- theatres and performing arts centers, ranging from a few hundred seats to much larger theatrical spaces.

Although the evening has changed in both musical and dramatic content—about seventy-five percent of the material is new each year—the basic purpose and aspiration of the show remains the same: to honor the season in song, story and poetry, to create an evening that begins the holidays, acknowledging the origin and wonder of that first Christmas season. The evening is created from a variety of sources - a collage of carols, songs, stories, poems, both old and new, traditional, modern, comic, passionate, historical and unusual, tales of and about the season. The show aspires to reveal, yet again, the mystery and spirit of the season, its celebration of renewal, of second chances, its drawing together of lost souls, the damaged, the frightened, the dismayed and desolate, all of us that make up the human experience, and bring them, once again, into that rich bond that we call… family. In all its forms.

An interwoven tapestry that warms and comforts each of us in the arms of family and community.

Looking around at the time of the first *Pudding*, it was difficult to find a Christmas evening that was neither a dramatization of *A Christmas Carol*, nor a Christmas concert of some kind, *A White Christmas* and *The Night Before*…or a pageant of the Nativity. For the most part it was either all Scrooge all the time, or intermittent processions of the three wise men in bathrobes carrying tiny boxes and perfume as gifts to the Holy Child with angels in white sheets and wire wings kneeling, singing "Away in a Manger." This was all to the good. But surely there was something else to be done for the season. As I thought about it then, I was sure that over the years I had encountered a wealth of material that was moving and deeply expressive, and ranged over a wide array of Christmas encounters and memories that struck to the very heart of this most extraordinary time. Of course, over time it became clear that there was a fortune of literary and musical gifts waiting be sung and said, tales to be told, lovely, moving, sad and funny, all dealing with Christmas by great authors from around the world — Shakespeare and Shaw, Mark Twain and Emily Dickinson, Longfellow, stories from every century since the birth of Jesus; tales of journeys and encounters, of family, friends and enemies, children lost and found again, Christmas dinners and puddings and exotic, bizarre recipes, and Christmas jokes. And of course the most extraordinary music, Mozart and Bach, Handel, and carols from all over the world-- a treasure of literary and musical gifts.

A Christmas Pudding, a recipe for a Christmas celebration...
The evening is simple, a story-telling evening graced with music. An evening to sit in candlelight amidst words and memories and dreams, bathed in great joyous music and to think, or perhaps dream, who we are in this season, who we have been and might become. It is a clean and elegant time in intention and it is possible, desirable even, to stage the event with great simplicity. A bare stage or raised platform, two podiums or music stands for the actor/ readers on either side of the stage, chairs on either side behind the podiums.

Chairs for a small choir can be placed either upstage center of the actors or downstage of the company, perhaps even on the floor below the stage -- a piano, candlelight and simple lighting for the three areas, Left, Center and Right.

That said, the show has played in a variety of settings—the splendor of a great and graceful church, the choir in robes against a gleaming Celtic cross, stained glass and velvet throws for the pulpits; in theatres, against the set of the current production but lavishly decorated with wreaths and brass candles, ornaments of every kind, a Christmas tree amidst a sweep of poinsettias and heaped 'presents'; on a tiny raised platform at a luncheon forum in a country club, bare stage, in full daylight. The material, music and text, has, infallibly, carried the day, transporting the audience into the spirit and heart of the season. It all works.

A Consort - Eight to twelve singers. Voices and musicianship as strong as you can get. Music selections will of course depend upon the skill and talent of the Consort and the amount of rehearsal time available. Selections made here are suggestions only and should be taken as a guide. The director and conductor of the Consort should feel free to make their own choices.

The music should be familiar yet unusual, living in our memory but not in the speakers of every elevator and department store. Of course, the best of Bach, Handel and Mozart, (assuming the chorus can handle the demands) are all available, a wealth of Christmas selections, though I would advise perhaps only a couple of selections of real challenge in each act. Traditional songs and carols, Irish, English, French, Russian, American 18th century—all of them work. Best is music that you've heard, but not for a while, and that you certainly won't hear on the annual television Christmas special. On this night, the audience usually doesn't need a 10th version of "Jingle Bells, or "Rudolph the Red Nose Reindeer" or the" Little Drummer Boy." But they might enjoy "The Holly and the Ivy" or "In the Bleak Midwinter" or "Il Est N'est."

Actors - Three men, three women, a range of ages, 20-35, 35-50, 50+. A range of voices, ages, attitudes. Ideally all of them should be able to handle challenging texts. Emily Dickinson, Longfellow, Dickens, Shaw, are not easy reads. All are demanding.

All require a level of skill, some ability to do character, accents, or a variety of tone and attitudes, that are best served with experience, rehearsal and hard work. Choose voices that are best suited for a particular story or poem.

A Note About the Actors and the Consort - Of course six actors and a Consort of eight to twelve is ideal. It may be, however, that a smaller group of actors and singers, might be necessary or even better for the presenting group.

If the actors can carry the additional weight in performance, it is conceivable that three actors might serve the production effectively; and as few as four singers, (soprano, alto, tenor, bass) again provided they serve the production and sustain its quality.

I would not recommend a company of fewer than three actors with a chorus of four singers.

Pace - It seems best if each act is played with a sustained energy or pace, with each piece, music or text, following immediately upon the next, no holding for applause, no break in the flow, each carol or poem or story, following on without a breath, as nearly as possible. The purpose is to use each selection as a comment or introduction to the one it proceeds or follows, to make its statement in the context of the evening and to move toward a cumulative result, each poem or carol building upon the next, enriching the spirit and substance of the mood and meaning of the act or evening. To that end, it seems best to discourage applause, to let the audience know immediately that the rhythm and pace of the evening is quick, bright, with no invitation for polite applause allowed, that the story of the evening is the priority.

Nothing, I think, exhausts an audience and its attention more than actors/ musicians strolling forward to read, arranging themselves, their material with elaborate theatricality, or pausing dramatically, modestly when they've finished as an unspoken invitation (or request) for applause. Once the ritual of applause for each and every piece is introduced, the delicate gift of attention and concentration is dissipated, destroyed. The tedious, polite round of applause saps an audience's energy as quickly as a bad performance. The evening is about the material, and the actors' and singers' performances in the material. Frequent applause can become an enormous and ongoing punctuation, lengthening the evening, undermining the spirit, the joy and sustained energy that helps create a fine performance.

Best to move the actors who are about to read following a choral piece, to the podiums left and right (if pieces follow quickly one upon the other), just as the chorus or consort is standing to sing. Thus the reading following the music can begin immediately, using the music as a kind of introduction to the piece, or comment upon what's being read.

'Entrances' of actors, or singers, their moving to the podium or stand, preparing to read or sing, while the audience waits, should be eliminated as far as possible.

The actors should not, with the exceptions noted, introduce the pieces or the authors, but begin quite straightforwardly as if they themselves were the author. I would suggest that titles and authors not be read at all, unless it is absolutely necessary that the audience understand who the speaker is or the context of his words.

ACT I

Prologue *The Bird of Dawning,* from *Hamlet* by William Shakespeare

Luke 2: 1-12

> **Music Procession** - *Ding Dong Merrily on High*
> **Bell Peal**

Oh, Noisey Bells Be Dumb by John Skinner
An Atrocious Institution by George Bernard Shaw
A Christmas Letter by Stephen Leacock

> **Music**

Yes, Virginia There is a Santa Claus by Francis P. Church
A Letter from Santa Claus by Mark Twain

> **Music**

The Gift of the Magi by O. Henry

> **Music**

The First Day of Winter by Mollie Birney
Take Joy by Fra Giovanni

> **Music**

Midnight Mass by David Birney

INTERMISSION

ACT II

> **Music** - *Greensleeves*

A Christmas Carol Anonymous
King Arthur's Christmas by Sir Thomas Malory

> **Music**

The Finest Feast Anonymous
Fruitcake Recipe Anonymous

Music

The Savior must have been a Docile Gentleman by Emily Dickinson
Christmas Bells by Henry Wadsworth Longfellow

Music

The Star Next Door by A. J. Carothers

Music

First Day of Winter by Mollie Birney
Mistletoe by Walter de la Mare

Music - *London Waits*

From *A Christmas Carol* by Charles Dickens
    Scrooge and the Phantom
        London Waits or *Il Est Né,* one verse
    Christmas Morning
        London Waits or *Il Est Né,* one verse

    A Merry Christmas, Bob

Music - *Christmas is a Comin' The Goose is Getting Fat*

God Bless Us Every One by Charles Dickens

Luke 2: 12-14

Music - *We Wish You a Merry Christmas* or *Joy to the World*

A CHRISTMAS PUDDING

ACT I

(ENTER the first ACTOR, simply, moving quickly to a position among the audience, if possible, certainly on the forestage or if sightlines permit, down onto the floor in the first few rows. A spotlight, if available, or low light spreading to include the second ACTOR, and gradually growing brighter as the CONSORT ENTERS. He begins, casually, strolling perhaps down the center aisle, or moving L to R on a forestage, addressing the audience directly and intimately.)

HAMLET (Act I, Scene I) - William Shakespeare

(Again let me remind the actors that unless reading the title or the author of a piece to clarifies or illustrates a work, they should not be read.)

ACTOR. *(With great warmth, a bit of mystery, as well. It is the first gift of the evening — this "hallowed" and "gracious" time.)*

Some say that ever against
that season comes wherein
Our Saviour's birth is celebrated
the bird of dawning
singeth all night long.
And then, they say, no spirit
dare stir abroad.
No planet strikes.
No fairy takes nor witch
hath power to charm.
So hallowed and so
gracious is the time.

13

*(The FIRST ACTOR turns and faces a SECOND ACTOR who
has ENTERED quietly behind the FIRST ACTOR and is
now standing at the podium/stand SR. He begins immediately.)*

Luke II, Verses 1 - 12

SECOND ACTOR. (*Make the audience hear this as if it
were spoken for the very first time.*)

And it came to pass in those days, that there went out a de-
cree from Caesar Augustus, that all the world should be taxed.
And all went to be taxed, every one into his own city. And Jo-
seph also went up from Galilee, out of the city of Nazareth,
into Judea, unto the city of David, which is called Bethlehem;
because he was of the house and lineage of David; to be taxed
with Mary his espoused wife, being great with child.

And so it was, that, while they were there, the days were ac-
complished that she should be delivered. And she brought forth
her first born son, and wrapped him in swaddling clothes, and
laid him in a manger; because there was no room for them in
the inn.

And there were in the same country shepherds abiding in the
field, keeping watch over their flock by night. And, lo, the angel
of the Lord came upon them, and the glory of the Lord shone
round about them: and they were sore afraid. And the angel said
unto them, Fear not: for, behold, I bring you good tidings of
great joy, which shall be to all people. For unto you is born this

day in the city of David a Savior, which is Christ the Lord.

Music - Processional
"Hark the Herald Angels Sing," or
"Ding Dong Merrily on High"

(Processional begins immediately and the CONSORT ENTERS in procession. From wherever is most effective and efficient, proceeding, perhaps, down a Center aisle, or from either side of the wings Left and Right. They process, singing, toward their final places on stage in the order in which they will be seated. Final verse sung in place, all seated together with the last words of the verse.

ACTORS III, IV, V, and VI ENTER, at the same time as the CONSORT, either from Left and Right or opposite sides of the space. Those who will read next, "Oh, Noisey Bells Be Dumb" and "An Atrocious Institution" move to podiums SL and SR with a third actor who will read "A Christmas Letter" standing to the side and behind the actor who will read first, ready to step into his place as he finishes and as the actor begins "An Atrocious Institution." The remaining actors stand in front of their chairs and sit as the CONSORT sits.

Thus, there are three actors ready to read when the music finishes. The CONSORT and remaining actors sit as the BELL PEAL begins.

BELL PEAL. As "Hark the Herald" ENDS. The Chieftains have a 60-second bell peal that opens one of their albums. It is a wild, celebratory ringing out of the church bells of Dublin. It should be of that nature and length, immediately following the final verse sung by the Consort.)

Oh, Noisey Bells Be Dumb by John Skinner

ACTOR. *(At R podium. Playing off the bell peal, with some exasperation)*

Thursday, the 25th of December 1823
I cannot say my sleep was disturbed but my waking hours certainly were by the ringing of bells about 7 o'clock announcing the joyous day when half the parish at least will be drunk.

Tuesday, the 25th of December 1827
I was awakened early by the ringing of the bells and I could not help thinking how much sound overpowers common sense in all that we have to do in the present day. I lay awake last night thinking of these things and soon after I'd closed my eyes they were again opened by the loud peals these thoughtless people among whom I dwell choose to ring as they supposed in honor of the day. They had better retire within themselves and commune with their hearts and be still.

An Atrocious Institution by George Bernard Shaw

ACTOR. *(At L podium. Crisply, with passion. An Indictment.)* Like all intelligent people, I greatly dislike Christmas. It revolts me to see a whole nation refrain from music for weeks together in order that every man may rifle his neighbour's pockets under cover of a ghastly general pretence of festivity.

It is really an atrocious institution this Christmas.
We must become gluttonous because it is Christmas.

We must be drunken because it is Christmas.

We must be insincerely generous; we must buy things that nobody wants, and give them to people we don't like;

We must go to absurd entertainments that make even our little children satirical;

We must writhe under venal officiousness from legions of freebooters, all because it is Christmas—that is, because the mass of the population, including the all-powerful middle-class tradesman, depends on a week of license and brigandage, waste and intemperance, to clear off its outstanding liabilities at the end of the year.

George Bernard Shaw
(Actor should read Shaw's name.
In this instance it's probably better to read the author's name to
clarify who it is that has been speaking.)

A Christmas Letter by Stephen Leacock

ACTOR. Mademoiselle, allow me very gratefully but firmly to refuse your kind invitation. You doubtless mean well; but your ideas are unhappily mistaken.

You inform me that your maiden aunt intends to help you entertain the party. I have not, as you know, the honor of your aunt's acquaintance, yet I think I may with reason surmise that she will organize games – guessing games — in which she will ask me to name a river in Asia beginning with a Z; on my failure to do so she will put an ice cube down my neck as a penalty, and the children will clap their hands and laugh. These games, my dear young friend, involve the use of a more adaptable intellect than mine, and I cannot consent to be a party to them.

Neither can I look on with a complacent eye at the sad spectacle of your young clerical friend, the Reverend Mr. Uttermost Farthing, abandoning himself to such gambols and appearing in the role of life and soul of the evening. Such a degradation of his holy calling grieves me, and I cannot but suspect him of ulterior motives.

Let us understand one another once and for all. I cannot at my mature age participate in the sports of children with such abandon as I could wish. I entertain, and have always entertained, the sincerest regard for such games as Hunt-the-Slipper and Blind-Man's Buff. But I have now reached a time of life, when, to have my eyes blindfolded and to have a powerful boy of ten hit me in the back with a hobby-horse and ask me to guess who hit me, provokes me to a fit of retaliation which could only culminate in reckless criminality. Nor can I cover my shoulders with a drawing-room rug and crawl round on my hands and knees under the pretence that I am a bear without a sense of personal insufficiency, which is painful to me.

May I say in conclusion that I do not consider a five-cent penwiper from the top branch of a Christmas tree any adequate compensation for the kind of evening you propose.

I have the honor to subscribe myself your humble servant.

(CONSORT STANDS. Actors for "Yes, Virginia" and for "A

*Letter from Santa Claus" move to podiums L and R ready
to read at finish of musical selection. ACTOR for "Yes,
Virginia" reading the introduction and the ACTOR reading
the editor's piece should be at opposite podiums, with the
ACTOR reading TWAIN standing to the side, ready to slip
into the introduction reader's slot as he finishes.)*

Music
"Tomorrow Shall Be My Dancing Day" or
"We'll Dress the House in Mistletoe"

(CONSORT sits.)

Yes, Virginia by Francis P. Church

ACTOR. (*Introduction*) In 1897, a little girl in New York
City named Virginia O'Hanlon asked her father whether there
really was a Santa Claus. Her father, rather on the spot, abdi-
cated that judgment by encouraging her to ask the editor of the
New York Sun. Her letter, which soon became famous, read:

"Dear Editor: I am eight years old. Some of my little friends say
there is no Santa Claus. Papa says, "If you see it in the *Sun*, it's
so." Please tell me the truth, is there a Santa?"

The Sun answered her letter with an editorial by Francis P.
Church that became equally famous, and was reprinted in the
Sun every Christmas until the newspaper ceased publication in
1950.

ACTOR. (*Editor's piece. Speak as if to VIRGINIA, simply,* *gently, without patronizing her. He/she believes what he says.)*

"Yes, Virginia, there is a Santa Claus. He exists as certainly as love and generosity and devotion exist, and you know that they abound and give to your life its highest beauty and joy. Alas! How dreary would be the world if there were no Santa Claus. It would be as dreary as if there were no Virginias. The most real things in the world are those that neither children nor men can see. Did you ever see fairies dancing on the lawn? Of course not, but that's no proof that they are not there. Nobody can conceive or imagine all the wonders that are unseen and un-seeable in the world. Thank God Santa Claus lives, and he lives forever. A thousand years from now, Virginia, nay, ten times 10,000 years from now, he will continue to make glad the heart of childhood."

A Letter from Santa Claus by Mark Twain

ACTOR. (*Simple rather than cute. Remember the letter, though addressed to Susie, was probably read to the entire family, children, mother and nurse. Twain, I'm sure, read it straight with his own deliberate, easy pace.)*

My dear Susie Clemens:
I have received and read all the letters which you and your little sister have written me by the hand of your mother and your nurses; I have also read those which you little people have writ-ten me with your own hands — for although you did not use any characters that are in grown peoples' alphabet, you used the characters that all children in all lands on earth and in the twin-kling stars use; and as all my subjects in the moon are children

and use no character but that, you will easily understand that I can read your and your baby sister's jagged and fantastic marks without any trouble at all. But I had trouble with those letters which you dictated through your mother and the nurse, for I am a foreigner and cannot read English writing well. You will find that I made no mistakes about the things which you and the baby ordered in your own letters - I went down your chimney at midnight when you were asleep and delivered them all myself — and kissed both of you, too, because you are good children, well trained, nice mannered, and about the most obedient little people I ever saw.

Mark Twain
(Read the signature.
ACTORS sit as the CONSORT stands to sing. ACTOR for "The
Gift of the Magi" moves into position.)

Music
"Sussex Carol" or *"What Cheer?"* by William Walton

The Gift of the Magi by O. Henry

ACTOR. One dollar and eighty-seven cents. That was all. And sixty cents of it was in pennies. Pennies saved one and two at a time by bulldozing the grocer and the vegetable man and the butcher until one's cheeks burned. Three times Della counted it. One dollar and eighty-seven cents. And the next day would be Christmas.

There was clearly nothing to do but flop down on the shabby little couch and howl. So Della did it. Life is made up of sobs, sniffles, and smiles, with sniffles predominating.

While the mistress of the home subsides into sniffles, let's take a look at the home. A furnished flat at $8 per week.

In the vestibule below was a letter-box into which no letter would go, and an electric button from which no mortal finger could coax a ring. There was a card bearing the name "Mr. James Dillingham Young."

The "Dillingham" had been flung to the breeze during a former period of prosperity when its possessor was being paid $30 per week. Now, when the income was shrunk to $20, though, they were thinking seriously of contracting to a modest and unassuming D. But whenever Mr. James Dillingham Young came home and reached his flat above he was called "Jim" and greatly hugged by Mrs. James Dillingham Young, Della, as you know. Which is all very good.

Della finished her cry and attended to her cheeks with powder. She stood by the window and looked out dully at a gray cat walking a gray fence in a gray backyard. Tomorrow would be Christmas Day, and she had only $1.87 with which to buy Jim a present. She had been saving every penny she could for months, with this result. Twenty dollars a week doesn't go far. Expenses had been greater than she had calculated. They always are. Only $1.87 to buy a present for Jim. Her Jim. Many a happy hour she had spent planning for something nice for him. Something fine and rare and sterling--something worthy of the honor of being married to Jim.

Suddenly Della whirled from the window and stood before the mirror. Her eyes were shining brilliantly, but her face had lost its color within twenty seconds. Rapidly she pulled down her hair and let it fall to its full length.

Now, there were two possessions of the James Dillingham Young's in which they both took a mighty pride. One was Jim's gold watch that had been his father's and his grandfather's. The other was Della's hair. Had the queen of Sheba lived in the flat across the airshaft, Della would have let her hair hang out the window some day to dry just to depreciate Her Majesty's jewels and gifts. Had King Solomon been the janitor, with all his treasures piled up in the basement, Jim would have pulled out his watch every time he passed, just to see him pluck at his beard from envy.

So now Della's beautiful hair fell about her rippling and shining like a cascade of brown waters. It reached below her knee and made itself almost a garment for her. And then she did it up again nervously and quickly. Once she faltered for a minute and stood still while a tear or two splashed on the worn red carpet.

On went her old brown jacket; on went her old brown hat. With a whirl of skirts and with the brilliant sparkle still in her eyes, she fluttered out the door and down the stairs to the street.

Where she stopped the sign read: "Madame. Sofronie. Hair Goods of All Kinds." One flight up Della ran, and collected herself, panting. Madame, large, too white, chilly, hardly looked like her namesake, The Saint.

"Will you buy my hair?" asked Della.

"I buy hair," said Madame. "Take yer hat off and let's have a

sight at the looks of it."
Down rippled the brown cascade.

"Twenty dollars," said Madame, lifting the mass with a practiced hand.

"Give it to me quick," said Della.

Oh, and the next two hours flew by on rosy wings. She was ransacking the stores for Jim's present.

She found it at last. It surely had been made for Jim and no one else. There was no other like it in any of the stores, and she had turned all of them inside out. It was a platinum fob chain simple and chaste in design, proclaiming its value by substance alone—as all good things should do. It was even worthy of The Watch. As soon as she saw it she knew that it must be Jim's. It was like him. Quietness and value—the description applied to both. Twenty-one dollars they took from her for it, and she hurried home with the 87 cents. With that chain on his watch Jim might be properly anxious about the time in any company. Grand as the watch was, he sometimes looked at it on the sly on account of the old leather strap that he used in place of a chain.

When Della reached home her intoxication gave way to prudence and reason. She got out her curling irons and lighted the gas and went to work repairing the ravages made by generosity added to love. Which is always a tremendous task, friends—a mammoth task.

Within forty minutes her head was covered with tiny, close-lying curls that made her look wonderfully like a truant school-boy. She looked at her reflection in the mirror long, carefully, and critically.

"If Jim doesn't kill me," she said to herself, "before he takes a second look at me, he'll say I look like a Coney Island chorus girl. But what could I do—oh! what could I do with a dollar and eighty-seven cents?"

At 7 o'clock the coffee was made and the frying-pan was on the back of the stove hot and ready to cook the chops.

Jim was never late. Della doubled the fob chain in her hand and sat on the corner of the table near the door that he always entered. Then she heard his step on the stair down on the first flight, and she turned white for just a moment. She had a habit for saying little silent prayer about the simplest everyday things, and now she whispered: "Please God, make him think I am still pretty."

The door opened and Jim stepped in and closed it. He looked thin and very serious. Poor fellow, he was only twenty-two—and to be burdened with a family! He needed a new overcoat and he was without gloves.

Jim stopped inside the door, as immovable as a setter at the scent of quail. His eyes were fixed upon Della, and there was an expression in them that she could not read, and it terrified her. It was not anger, nor surprise, nor disapproval, nor horror, nor any of the sentiments that she had been prepared for. He simply stared at her fixedly with that peculiar expression on his face.

Della wriggled off the table and went for him.

"Jim, darling," she cried, "don't look at me that way. I had my hair cut off and sold because I couldn't have lived through Christmas without giving you a present. It'll grow out again--you won't mind, will you? I just had to do it. My hair grows awfully fast. Say 'Merry Christmas!' Jim, and let's be happy. You don't know what a nice--what a beautiful, nice gift I've got for you."

"You've cut off your hair?" asked Jim, laboriously, as if he had not arrived at that patent fact yet even after the hardest mental labor.

"Cut it off and sold it," said Della. "Don't you like me just as well, anyhow? I'm me without my hair, ain't I?"

Jim looked about the room curiously.

"You say your hair is gone?" he said, with an air almost of idiocy.

"You needn't look for it," said Della. "It's sold, I tell you--sold and gone, too. It's Christmas Eve, boy. Be good to me, for it went for you. Maybe the hairs of my head were numbered," she went on with sudden serious sweetness, "but nobody could ever count my love for you. Shall I put the chops on, Jim?"

Out of his trance Jim seemed quickly to wake. He enfolded his Della.

Jim drew a package from his overcoat pocket and threw it upon the table.

"Don't make any mistake, Dell," he said, "about me. I don't think there's anything in the way of a haircut or a shave or a shampoo that could make me like my girl any less. But if you'll unwrap that package you may see why you had me going a while at first."

White fingers and nimble tore at the string and paper. And then an ecstatic scream of joy; and then, alas! a quick feminine change to hysterical tears and wails, necessitating the immediate employment of all the comforting powers of the lord of the flat.

For there lay The Combs—the set of combs, side and back, that Della had worshipped long in a Broadway window. Beautiful combs, pure tortoise shell, with jewelled rims—just the shade to wear in the beautiful vanished hair. They were expensive combs, she knew, and her heart had simply craved and yearned over them without the least hope of possession. And now, they were hers, but the tresses that should have adorned the coveted adornments were gone.

But she hugged them to her bosom, and at length she was able to look up with dim eyes and a smile and say: "My hair grows so fast, Jim!"

And then Della leaped up like a little singed cat and cried, "Oh, oh!"

Jim had not yet seen his beautiful present. She held it out to him eagerly upon her open palm. The dull precious metal seemed to flash with a reflection of her bright and ardent spirit.

"Isn't it a dandy, Jim? I hunted all over town to find it. You'll have to look at the time a hundred times a day now. Give me your watch. I want to see how it looks on it."

Instead of obeying, Jim tumbled down on the couch and put his hands under the back of his head and smiled.

"Dell," said he, "let's put our Christmas presents away and keep 'em a while. They're too nice to use just at present. I sold the watch to get the money to buy your combs. And now suppose you put the chops on."

The magi, as you know, were wise men--wonderfully wise men—who brought gifts to the Babe in the manger. They invented the art of giving Christmas presents. Being wise, their gifts were no doubt wise ones, possibly bearing the privilege of exchange in case of duplication. And here I have related to you the uneventful chronicle of two foolish children in a flat who most unwisely sacrificed for each other the greatest treasures of their house. But in a last word to the wise of these days let it be said that of all who give gifts these two were the wisest. Of all who give and receive gifts, such as they are wisest. Everywhere they are wisest. They are the magi.

(CONSORT STANDS as ACTORS for "The First Day of Winter" and "Take Joy" move to L and R podiums.)

Music
"Coventry Carol" or "God Rest Ye Merry Gentlemen"

(CONSORT SITS.)

First Day of Winter by Mollie Birney

ACTOR. (*It is the girl's voice, but in memory. Simple is best. Women of different ages, from 15-75, will have their own take on the poem and the memory.*)

I remember skating on the rink
just inside the park.
I remember grandpa
sitting alone on a nearby park bench
watching me.

I remember snow angels
we had made
lying next to him in the slush.
I remember the tired old trees
that encircled the rink
bowing and bending with the wind.

I remember the snow
on my new pink mittens,
and being upset with myself for soiling them,
and not staying up on my new skates
like I had hoped to.

I remember the Christmas lights
that wound around and around
the nearby lampposts
that my brother and I
had accidentally sledded into
the day before.

I remember forgetting
just where I had put my shoes
before I began to skate
and having to walk home
with Grandpa's
mittens on my feet.
That was the day
when I first understood
why winter was so special.

Take Joy by Fra Giovanni, 1513

    ACTOR. There is nothing I can give you
    Which you have not,
But there is much, very much that
    while I cannot give it, you can take.

No heaven can come to us unless our hearts find rest today,
    Take heaven!
No peace lives in the future which is not hidden in this present
instant.
    Take Peace!

The gloom of the world is but a shadow.
Behind it, yet within reach is joy.
There is a radiance and glory in the darkness,
could we but see, and to see we have only to look.
I beseech you to look.

Life is so generous a giver, but we,
judging its gifts by their covering, cast them away

as ugly, or heavy, or hard.
Remove the covering and you will find beneath it,
a living splendor, woven of love, by wisdom, with power.

Welcome it, grasp it and you touch the angel's hand
that brings it to you. Everything we call a trial, a sorrow or a
duty, Believe me, that angel's hand is there; the gift is there,
and the wonder of an overshadowing Presence.
Our joys, too:
Be not content with them as joys;
They too conceal divine gifts.

And so, at this time, I greet you.
Not quite as the world sends greetings,
But with profound esteem
And the prayer that for you, now and forever,
The day breaks and the shadows flee away.

*(CONSORT STANDS. ACTOR for "Midnight Mass" moves to
    podium.)*

Music
"The Holly and the Ivy" or *"Ding, Dong Merrily on High"*

(CONSORT SITS.)

Midnight Mass by David Birney

ACTOR. For the last dozen years or so I have sung in
the choir at Midnight Mass at St. Mary's Catholic Church on
Christmas Eve in Park City, Utah. I am neither a Catholic, nor

a member of any organized choir or choral group, and yet this Christmas Eve event, by now nearly a ritual, is one of the most joyous and moving experiences of my Christmas season.

It is a small, plain church of clapboard and plaster, a functional altar attended by a single altar boy, several rows of pews separated by a center aisle. Tiny by any standard, the church seats, I would imagine, barely a hundred. A miniscule choir loft with almost enough room for an old upright piano and a gaggle of folding chairs perches atop a narrow, crooked flight of stairs at the rear of the building.

The priest, Father Ryan, is a relatively young, vulnerable looking Irishman whose ministry this has been for the past twelve years or so. It is rumored that this may be his final Christmas in this parish, a fact he seems to accept with reluctant grace.

The crowd on Christmas Eve is nearly double the capacity of the cramped structure and the temperature, though below zero outside, soars into the tropical range during the service. Nevertheless, a kind of high Dickensian spirit prevails and that, plus, no doubt, the alcoholic residue of various pre-Mass parties, combine to create an atmosphere of festive but hushed expectation broken occasionally by exclamations of joyous greeting or shared laughter. It is unexpectedly a community, a community already bound together in surprise at finding itself gathered in this tiny church in the mountains. They are good humored and somehow faintly astonished, awaiting what? probably not blessing or grace, but something much simpler, an obligation fulfilled perhaps, the day marked, the season sung; perhaps being together is enough.

With me in the loft are two of my older children (the babies are home, long asleep), another family with whom we are very close, ten or twelve locals who are regular members of the choir, and a straggle of visitors from out of town, or around town, some sober, some not, who happen to be here for the holidays. The "choir" is led by the former editor of the local paper (let's call him Jerry), a bright and funny man who is usually well fortified before his arrival by several seasonal toasts to the success of the evening, and who insures the continuity of that fortification with the aid of a flask forthrightly present on the upright piano. This past year Jerry retired and moved to Boston, but he has flown in tonight to honor an old obligation and we are glad to see him.

He directs passionately, if unconventionally. Each selection is begun with a thunderous *sotto voce* exhortation to, "Hit it!" And this square stocky man with the sweaty fervent face, eyes closed, does indeed, "Hit it!" his entire body wringing the rhythm and dynamic of the hymn from the close and humid air. It is an extraordinary performance, not at all musical in its aggressive athleticism; it is comic, ironic, and yet deeply committed and, in some final sense, joyous...religious. We would probably follow him off the balcony if he asked.

We are, ourselves, a fairly motley crew, distinguished by our passion to sing rather than our musical abilities. On this night the service is prefaced by a medley of carols in rough (oh, very rough, indeed) harmony, each carol prefaced by much whispered instruction... "Only the first and third verses!' "Which verses?" "THE FIRST AND THIRD!" Much rustling and page turning of the mimeographed handouts of "Twenty Popu-

lar Songs of the Christmas Season,... "What page is it on?"
"We Three Kings?' "NO, GOOD KING WENCESLAS"...
and bursts of suppressed laughter when one of the baritones
whose cup overfloweth comes to "adore Him" a full measure
too soon.

More than once we are gently reminded by Father Ryan this
night to "keep our feet firmly planted on the rock of reverence,"
and "to serve the spirit of the service." Father Ryan has a passion for alliteration. There has apparently been some miscom-
munication between Jerry and Father Ryan as we are led (Well,
"led" is not quite the word. "Driven" might do, or perhaps even
"wrestled.") through five (count 'em) renditions of "Adeste Fi-
deles," three verses each, expecting each time the entrance of
the processional on the first words of the final verse. By the
third attempt the congregation is more than a little puzzled; by
the fourth, confusion reigns. The fifth repeat of "Oh Come All
You Faithful" finds many of those same faithful doubled up with
laughter and small children have begun to cry. Father Ryan and
the altar boy enter, finally, in the bewildered silence following
the final, "Chri-ist, the Lord!"   We collapse in various attitudes
of exhausted gratitude. This, I might add, is the kind of event
that is not at all unusual in the course of the evening.

The "choir" originated a dozen years ago in the saloon of one of
the local hotels on the night before Christmas Eve. Father Ryan,
then newly ordained and still a stranger to the community, over
a beer wondered aloud to the bartender how he was to conduct
a Christmas service with only the support of an elderly pianist
and a young woman who, in the spirit of the sixties, played
three chords on a guitar and whose entire repertoire seemed

to consist of, "Michael Row the Boat Ashore," and "Puff the Magic Dragon." The bartender was Jerry.

The next night at 11: 45 p.m. fourteen regulars from the bar, male and female, in boots and jeans and heavy sweaters and parkas, members of the ski patrol, construction workers, a real estate salesman and two service station attendants, their wives, husbands, girlfriends and various others led by Jerry, entered the little church and thundered their way up the crooked staircase to the loft, seated themselves, and burst into a lively, if somewhat tuneless version of, "We Wish You a Merry Christmas." Though the composition of the choir continues to change from year to year the tradition has continued, and tonight the loft overflows with latecomers singing from the stairwell.

The service is brief, centered on the celebration of the Mass and, for the most part, goes off without incident. The little girl carrying the Baby Jesus almost drops him as his blanket comes undone but in a swift, acrobatic move, she catches him by his foot and lays him tenderly, so tenderly, in the manger underneath the single unornamented pine tree. The guitar solo ("Oh Holy Night") remains for the most part on key and the choir gathers its limited resources for a joyously harmonized version of "Joy to the World," the basses sounding particularly robust and rugged in the "while fields and floods, rocks, hills and plains... repeat the sounding joy" section. There is a poignant resonance to the Mass this evening, Father Ryan turning to the congregation, raising the Host high above his head for what we realize may be the last time in this smallest of churches almost hidden in the snow- steeped mountains. The Mass in his Irish-inflected English has a kind of tender majesty this night.

Traditionally, the service ends with each of us holding a single candle. While the choir sings "Silent Night," the lights are turned off and a flame is passed along each row of the congregation from front to back until the entire church is alive with the shimmering light from these massed candles. At that point everyone joins in singing the final verse of the carol. Tonight, however, that ritual is to be altered. Jerry has somehow convinced Father Ryan to sing the verse in Gaelic, and then we are to join together for a last verse. It is to be a kind of tribute to the unique contribution of this gentle priest from across the sea to the life of this mountain community.

All seems to go as planned, the gentle sound of the hymn accompanying a growing body of light. The choir finishes its verse and looks toward Father Ryan. It is very still.

He begins. The first words are strange, unexpectedly shaped and jarring. They grow jagged, broken, crumbling slowly. We are puzzled. What does he sing? What does he say? What is gradually apparent is that it is not the language that jars but the simple fact that he is completely, irrevocably, in the wrong key, in fact in no key at all, a realization that comes slowly to us all but to him in a sudden and terrible burst of humiliation. His voice, so melodic in the Mass, breaks and crumbles as the syllables grind against one another and fall individually into silence...a terrible silence. He seems somehow completely beyond our reach, our help, as if he were suddenly at a great distance, a distance beyond sound or speech, or as if a wall of thick and impenetrable glass had fallen around him, locking him from his people, his family.

The quiet thunders. The light wavers on the faces of each of us, and Father Ryan smiles briefly and tries to speak...and stops. He stands with head bowed, gazing at the floor as if caught in a terrible dream.

Somewhere a single voice, a woman's voice, begins to hum, "Silent Night." It is a small voice, thin but with a kind of fiber to it, persistent, it carries high above the dimly lit faces below. In time, it is joined by another voice and then several others, steady, building, a stream of melody, and finally all of us together, joined in a kind of sea of simple song, the old hymn as strong as an ocean. Father Ryan joins us, tentatively at first, but bolder, brighter, in tune, the Gaelic words rising above and buoyed by the flow of melody like a brave craft upon the waves. We come through the voyage together, finishing the carol as if coming home to shore, joined in a gathering of heart and quick joy at our common triumph, joyous in our relief at rediscovering the strength uncovered in the gesture of one being reaching out to another. And how just and fitting that Father Ryan should have been on this night, this last night, the instrument of that ageless lesson, that secret of this most mysterious season.

As I leave the church the stars seem still and serene in the blackest of midnight skies. I am glad that my children have been with me this night.

INTERMISSION

ACT II

(ACTORS ENTER, the two who are to read going to podiums L and R. The other ACTORS sit. THE CONSORT follows and crosses to Center and remain standing, ready to sing.)

Music
"Greensleeves" or *"Psallite"* by Michael Praetorius

(CONSORT SITS.)

A Christmas Carol, 16th Century, Anonymous

ACTOR.
The other night, I saw a light,
A star as bright as day,
And ever among an angel sung,
"Bye Bye Baby, Lullay."

A virgin clear, who had no peer
Unto her son did say,
"I pray thee, son, grant me a boon,
To sing Bye Bye Lullay."

Let child or man, Whoever can,
Be merry on this day,
And blessing bring to Christ, our King,
Bye Bye Baby, Lullay.

(CONSORT SITS.)

King Arthur's Christmas by Sir Thomas Malory

ACTOR. (*There is an archaic formality to the piece that requires an Actor who is comfortable with language and can make it accessible and natural.*)

Then Merlin went to the Archbishop of Canterbury, and counseled him for to send for all the lords of the Realm, and all the gentlemen of arms, that they should come to London by Christmas, upon pain of cursing and for this cause, that Jesus that was born on that night, would of his great mercy shew some miracle, as he was come to be king of mankind, to shew who would be rightful king of this realm. So the Archbishop, by the advice of Merlin, sent for all the Lords that they should come by Christmas unto London. And make of them clean of their life (shriven by a priest in the sacrament of Confession), that their prayer might be more acceptable to God…And when matins and the First Mass of Christmas was done, there was seen in the churchyard, against the High Altar, a great stone four square… and therein stuck a fair sword…and letters where were written in gold about the stone that said thus: Whoso pulleth out this sword of this stone and anvil, is rightwise king born of all England…But none might stir the sword nor use it…

So upon New Year's Day, when the service was done, the barons rode unto the field, some to joust, some to tourney, and so it happened that Sir Ector rode unto the joust, and with him rode Sir Kay his son, and young Arthur that was his nourished brother…Sir Kay lost his sword for he had left it at his father's lodging, and so he prayed young Arthur to ride for his sword… Then Arthur said to himself, I will take the sword that sticketh in the stone...so he handled the sword by the handles, and lightly and fiercely pulled it out from the stone...and rode his way until he came to Sir Kay and delivered him the sword. Sir Kay saw the sword and knew it well as the sword in the stone... therewithal they went unto the archbishop, and told him how the sword was achieved, and by whom; and on Twelfth-Day all the barons came thither, and to try to take the sword, who that would try. But there afore them all there might none take it out but Arthur.

Music

(CONSORT RISES to sing. ACTORS for "The Finest Feast" and "Fruitcake Recipe" move to podiums.)

"What Child is This" or *"In the Bleak Midwinter"*

(CONSORT SITS.)

The Finest Feast **Anonymous, 1814**

ACTOR. (*This woman or man is passionate about this recipe. She loves it. It is her absolute best for holiday entertaining. She is perhaps a tiny bit insane. She enjoys reading the recipe almost as much as eating the result. Don't rush but never falter.*)

Take a large olive, stone it and then stuff it with a paste made of anchovy, capers and oil. Put the olive inside a trussed and boned beck fig. Put the beck fig inside a fat ortolan. Put the ortolan inside a boned lark. Put the stuffed lark inside a boned thrush. Put the thrush inside a fat quail. Put the quail, wrapped in vine leaves, inside a boned lapwing. Put the lapwing inside a boned golden plover. Put the plover inside a fat, boned red-legged partridge. Put the partridge inside a young, boned and well-hung woodcock. Put the woodcock, rolled in bread crumbs, inside a boned teal. Put the teal inside a boned guinea-fowl. Put the guinea-fowl, well-larded, inside a young and boned tame duck. Put the duck inside a boned and fat pow. Put the pow inside a well-hung pheasant. Put the pheasant inside a boned and fat wild goose. Put the goose inside a pined turkey. Put the turkey inside a boned bustard. Having arranged your roast after this fashion, place it in a large saucepan with onions stuffed with cloves, carrots, small squares of ham, celery, minionette, several strips of bacon (well-seasoned), pepper, salt, spice, coriander seeds and two cloves of garlic. Seal the saucepan hermetically by closing it with pastry. Then put it for ten hours over a dreadful fire and arrange it so that the heat can penetrate evenly. An oven moderately heated will suit better than the hearth. Before serving, remove the pastry, put the roast on a hot dish after having removed the grease if there is any, and serve.

Fruitcake Recipe Anonymous

ACTOR. (*This character is oddly innocent and a bit uncomfortable about reading this recipe. He's not quite sure where he is or why he's been asked to read it. He never anticipates the result of each new ingredient or action. Not a clue. So the recipe overtakes him, rather his making it happen. Everything, including what he's just said, surprises him. And sometimes, perhaps, makes him laugh inappropriately. He is unaware of his growing drunkenness until he IS absolutely bombed. Then he's immortal. Hugely bombed. Enjoy it. Good luck.*)

Fruitcake Recipe
(Read this title as if it were your own recipe.)

1 cup water
1 cup sugar
4 large eggs
2 cups dried fruit
1 teaspoon baking soda
1 teaspoon salt
1 cup brown sugar
lemon juice
nuts
1 gallon whiskey

Sample the whiskey to check for quality.
Tak a large bowl.
Check the whiskey again to be sure it is of the highest quality.
Pour one level cup and drink.
Repeat.
Turn on the electric mixer; beat 1 cup butter in a large, fluffy
      bowl.
Add 1 teaspoon sugar and beat again.
Make sure the whiskey is still OK. Cry another tup. Turn off
      mixer.
Break 2 legs and add to the bowl and chuck in the cup of dried
      fruit.
Mix on the turner.
If the fried druit gets stuck in the beaterers, pry it loose with a
      drewscriver.
Sample the whiskey to check for tonsisticity.
Next, sift 2 cups of salt. Or something.

Who cares?
Check the whiskey.
Now sift the lemon juice and strain your nuts.
Add one table. Spoon. Of sugar or something.
Whatever you can find.
Grease the oven.
Turn the cake tin to 350 degrees.
Don't forget to beat off the turner.
Throw the bowl out of the window.
Check the whiskey again.
Go to bed.
Who the hell likes fruitcake anyway?

(CONSORT RISES to sing. ACTORS for "The Savior Must Have Been a Docile Gentleman" and "Christmas Bells" move to podiums L and R.)

Music
"Go Tell It on the Mountain" or
"God Rest Ye Merry Gentlemen"

(CONSORT SITS.)

The Savior must have been a Docile Gentleman
by Emily Dickinson

ACTOR. (*Dickinson is a tough poet, tough minded, harder and more durable than her popular image…it's not a hundred, a thousand, a million, but a "rugged billion Miles."*)

The Savior must have been

A docile Gentleman—
To Come so far so cold a Day
For little Fellowmen.

The road to Bethlehem
Since He and I were Boys
Was leveled. But for that 'twould be
A rugged billion Miles.

Christmas Bells by Henry Wadsworth Longfellow

ACTOR. (*Keep in mind that the cannons in the poem
are not metaphor or generic cannons, they are the cannons of
Gettysburg, of Antioch and Atlanta, the great bloody battles
of our tragic Civil War. The narrator's despair is profound as
the "hearths" and "households" of the nation are mocked by
"hate." The redemption of the Christmas bells is not sentimen-
tal. It is profound and profoundly felt.*)

I Heard the bells on Christmas Day,
Their old, familiar carols play,
        And wild and sweet
        The words repeat
Of peace on earth, good-will to men!

And thought how, as the day had come,
The belfries of all Christendom
        Had rolled along
        The unbroken song
Of peace on earth, good-will to men!

Till, ringing, singing on its way,
The world revolved from night to day,
A voice, a chime
A chant sublime
Of peace on earth, good-will to men!

Then from each black, accursed mouth
The cannon thundered in the south,
And with the sound
The carols drowned
Of peace on earth, good-will to men!

It was as if an earthquake rent
The hearth-stones of a continent,
And made forlorn
The households born
Of peace on earth, good-will to men!

And in despair i bowed my head;
"There is no peace on earth," i said;
"For hate is strong;
And mocks the song
Of peace on earth, good-will to men!"

Then pealed the bells more loud and deep:
"God is not dead; nor doth he sleep!
The wrong shall fail,
The right prevail,
With peace on earth, good-will to men!"

*(CONSORT STANDS ready to sing. ACTOR moves to podium
     L or R to read.)*

Music
"The Star Carol" by Alfred Burt or
"What Child Is This?"

The Star Next Door by A. J. Carothers

ACTOR. (*The narrator, though grown, is recalling a time,
a Christmas Eve, when he was eight years old. He is an only
child who "went everywhere with his parents," and who on this
particular night suffers a great loss; one of those losses that
constitute a betrayal of the heart, of faith, of innocence, and begins a journey into the inevitable pain of the world's tragic nature. There is fragility in this voice, not indulged, simply there.
And a resilience.*

*On a practical note, it might be of use to remember that in that
time and place, Houston 1942, the world of this boy, the am-
biance is probably more southern than the popular cliché of
swaggering rawhide chaps and saddle Texas with which we
have grown familiar.)*

I heard this sound, this roar. Distant. Familiar. A prop plane!
No sound like it. The roar grew louder. Maybe a multi-engine
prop plane. The kind I first flew in, on my way from Houston
to Dallas for a football game. I looked up. Directly overhead,
four P-40's, in close formation, relics of World War II. It took
me back to my childhood. To another world, where right was
right and wrong was wrong, and it felt good to be on the right

side, knowing heroes were defending me.

I remembered the first time I saw P-40's, or any other fighter plane. A whole squadron was passing over my hometown, flying low, thundering overhead. I almost fell off my bike.

Houston wasn't a small town in 1942 – maybe a quarter of a million people – but it felt small to me, as I lived in just one of its corners, where family and friends and school were all at hand. Except on Thursday nights, when my mother and father -- he having been picked up from his office downtown – had dinner at the Forum Cafeteria and went to a picture show. Where they went, I went. If there was such a thing as a babysitter at that time and place, my parents never employed one. I could go to a movie for twelve cents. What would a babysitter cost? Half a dollar, maybe. I loved the movies. There were a lot of fighter planes in the pictures we saw.

The P-40's that scared me so were courtesy of Ellington Field, a base built by the Army Air Corps some miles southwest of town, on the Galveston road. After the first shock of hearing that roar, I was thrilled, seeing those planes overhead and thinking about Phil Jander, who lived next door and had gone off to fly P-40's in the South Pacific.

I didn't know many people who had gone off to war. My father was still a civilian. He called me his weather-stripping, because I kept him out the draft. The fact is, he turned 38 in 1942, so he was too old to be called up. And a few friends of my family had gone, but it didn't really register, because I didn't miss them. I missed Phil Jander.

He was eighteen years old, which made him ten years my senior. But he never ignored me, the way older people often did. Sometimes, we played catch with the special baseball he had snagged at a Buffalos game -- that was the name of our minor-league team, the Houston Buffalos – when somebody hit a high pop fly that Phil was quick enough to catch. He said it was a lucky ball and he was taking it off to war with him. I got reports on Phil whenever a V-mail arrived from wherever he was stationed – of course, we couldn't know. Mrs. Jander would tell me things he wrote and I felt close to him. He was my own personal hero.

It was Christmas Eve when the P-40's flew over, an early present. At church that night, I asked God to watch over all the planes and the pilots who flew them, especially Phil Jander. My parents were not churchgoers. I was, by choice. So, on that Christmas Eve, I walked home by myself, past houses with decorated trees in the windows and in some, a little flag with a blue star that said someone from that house was in the service of his country. Feeling very much in touch with the spirit of the season, especially the miracle of that night so long ago, that birthday night, I searched the sky for an especially bright star. But they all looked about the same. Then, walking past the Janders' house, I saw something that made the heart jump in my skinny eight-year-old person. The blue star in their window had turned to gold. A miracle, right here, next door to my own home!

I rushed in the house to announce it to my parents. "I prayed really hard at church, and I guess an angel came to the Janders' house and turned Phil's star gold! It's a Christmas star, in their window!" My parents looked at each other in the strangest way.

I went on: "Do you think they know it? Maybe we ought to go over and ask them." Asking seemed like such a good idea, I started for the door.

"No!" my father barked. Then, in a softer voice, "Don't you know what a gold star means?"

My mother answered for me. "He's never seen one before. It's the first one in our neighborhood."

They looked at each other again, and I knew what it meant. They were silently debating which one would tell me something. After a long time, my father accepted the task, without saying a word, and my mother went off to the kitchen.

He explained that the gold star meant Phil had been killed in action. The telegram had been delivered while I was at church.

"That's a lie!" I said, and went to my room. Amazingly, my father did not follow, removing his belt. Calling him a liar would ordinarily have brought swift punishment. I was even more confused. Lying across my bed, I could see out the window at the Christmas Eve night. Was it possible? I had gone to church on this night that was all about being born and while I was there praying for my neighbor, he died? Would God do that? Would He trick me with a gold star?

When my mother came to see if I was all right, I told her I was never going to church again. I wasn't even going to say my prayers. It was over between me and God.

It was the next morning, Christmas morning, that the real miracle happened. When I woke up, groggy from a restless night, there, on the bed stand, was a baseball. I recognized the pattern of the stains.

I ran downstairs, the ball clutched in both my hands, to show my parents. How did Phil Jander's baseball get all the way from the South Pacific to my room in Houston, Texas? My parents said they had no idea. They seemed as puzzled as I.

I ran next door, still in my pajamas. Mrs. Jander was slow coming to the door and she looked very tired. I showed her the ball that had mysteriously appeared by my bed. She had no answer for me. She had thought Phil meant to take it with him. When I held it out to her — after all, it wasn't mine — she shook her head. Phil must have wanted me to have it. She gave me a hug that lasted longer than most hugs, and went back inside.

I went straight back to my room and said the prayers I had defiantly refused to say the night before. I told God I didn't like Him letting Phil die, but I guess He knew more than I did, about how things had to be. And I was glad He let Phil bring me his baseball on the way to heaven.

My parents never changed their story, maintaining that they didn't know how that baseball traveled halfway around the world. The Janders moved away soon after that Christmas, so I never had the chance, when I was older, to ask Mrs. Jander again. And, now that I am much older, I think it's better to not know, to leave it alone. God knows.

I don't think of Phil much anymore, though I still have that baseball somewhere. But today, when those P-40's flew over, it all came back. And you know what a P-40 carries on its tail? A star.

(CONSORT RISES to sing. ACTORS for "What Lies Behind the Darkness" and "Mistletoe" go to the podiums L and R)

Music
"The Star Carol" by Alfred Burt or *"Mistletoe"*

(CONSORT SITS.)

What Lies Behind The Darkness by Mollie Birney

ACTOR.
What lies behind the darkness,
What part of night can I not see?
The enigma that pours
inside the doors of deep eternity;
accented by the frigid lace,
the white menagerie.
The snow that blends with black,
The curtain pulled across my eyes,
I can no longer see
the miracle night now hides.

Mistletoe by Walter de la Mare

ACTOR. *(This is a most mysterious poem. Take time to set the mood, be careful with the details, the one last candle, the shadows, sleepy, lonely...and this still kiss. Is she dreaming?*

And is she kissed once…or twice?)

Sitting under the mistletoe
(Pale-green, fairy mistletoe),
One last candle burning low,
All the sleepy dancers gone,
Just one candle burning on,
Shadows lurking everywhere:
Some one came, and kissed me there.

Tired I was; my head would go
Nodding under the mistletoe
(Pale-green, fairy mistletoe),
No footsteps came, no voice, but only,
Just as I sat there, sleepy, lonely,
Stooped in the still and shadowy air
Lips unseen—and kissed me there.

(CONSORT STANDS ready to sing. ACTORS to podiums. Music here as an intro into the three parts of the Dickens, a verse leading into each part. The THIRD ACTOR slipping behind the podium as third verse is sung.)

Music
"London Waits" or *"Il Est Né"* (Two Verses)

(CONSORT SITS AFTER MUSIC.)

A Christmas Carol by Charles Dickens

(After THE CONSORT has sung the first two verses to introduce

the Dickens reading, they should sit and remain seated for the remainder of the Dickens. These should be sung quietly, lightly; the effect should be carolers at a distance in the night.

This selection from A Christmas Carol *by Charles Dickens can be read by a single voice, two voices or even three. Director's choice. It is, of course, [as Dickens himself proved] eminently actable, though a substantial challenge. The three pieces together require stamina, concentration and commitment. If three actors are used, some care should be taken to assure a narrative flow and a consistency of characterization.*

There are a number of characters to be read. Each of them needs to be a distinct voice, a specific character. They need not be elaborate, but they should be distinct, clear, swift and convincing.

That said, simplicity trumps over-dramatization. Less is more. Don't rush, but be aware of pace. The storyteller's pace around a fireplace at night.)

Scrooge and the Phantom

ACTOR. Scrooge and the Phantom left this busy scene, and went into an obscure part of the town, to a low shop where iron, old rags, bottles, bones and greasy offal were bought. A grey-haired rascal, of great age, sat smoking his pipe. They came into the presence of this man, just as a woman with a heavy bundle slunk into the shop.

"What have you got to sell? What have you got to sell?" said the man.

"Half a minute's patience, Joe, and you shall see. Here," she said, throwing the bundle on the floor. "Every person has a right to take care of themselves. *He* always did! Who's the worse for the loss of a few things like these? Not a dead man, I suppose. What? If he wanted to keep 'em after he was dead, a wicked old screw, why wasn't he natural in his lifetime? If he had been, he'd have had somebody to look after him when he was struck with Death, instead of lying gasping out his last there, alone by himself."

"It's the truest word that ever was spoke, it's a judgment on him."

Scrooge listened to this dialogue in horror.

"Spirit! I see, I see. The case of this unhappy man might be my own. My life tends that way, now. Merciful Heavens, what is this?"

The scene had changed, and now he almost touched a bare, un-curtained bed. A pale light, rising in the outer air, fell straight upon this bed; and on it, unwatched, unwept, uncared for, was the body of a plundered unknown man.

"Spirit, let me see some tenderness connected with this death, or this dark chamber, Spirit, will be for ever present to me."

He broke down all at once. He couldn't help it. "Spectre," said Scrooge, "something informs me that our parting moment is at hand. I know it, but I know not how. Tell me what man that was, with the covered face, whom we saw lying dead."

The Ghost of Christmas Yet to Come conveyed him to a dismal, wretched, ruinous churchyard. The Spirit stood amongst the graves, and pointed down to one.

"Before I draw nearer to that stone to which you point, answer me one question. Are these the shadows of the things that Will be, or are they shadows of the things that May be only?"

Still the Ghost pointed downward to the grave by which it stood.

"Men's courses will foreshadow certain ends, to which, if persevered in, they must lead. But if the courses be departed from, the ends will change. Say it is thus with what you show me!"

The Spirit was immovable as ever.

Scrooge crept towards it, trembling as he went; and, following the finger, read upon the stone of the neglected grave his own name – Ebenezer Scrooge.

"Am I that man who lay upon the bed? No, Spirit! Oh no, no! Spirit! Hear me! I am not the man I was. I will not be the man I must have been but for this intercourse. Why show me this, if I am past all hope? Assure me that I yet may change these shadows you have shown me by an altered life."

"I will honour Christmas in my heart, and try to keep it all the year. I will live in the Past, the Present, and the Future. The Spirits of all three shall strive within me. I will not shut out the lessons that they teach. Oh, tell me I may sponge away the writing on this stone!"

Holding up his hands in one last prayer to have his fate reversed, Scrooge saw an alteration in the Phantom's hood and dress.

(CONSORT REMAINS SEATED.)

Music
"London Waits" or *"Il Est Né"* **(One verse)**

Christmas Morning

ACTOR. Holding up his hands in one last prayer to have his fate reversed, Scrooge saw an alteration in the Phantom's hood and dress. It shrunk, collapsed, and dwindled down into a bedpost.

Yes, and the bedpost was his own. The bed was his own, the room was his own. Best and happiest of all, the Time before him was his own, to make amends in!

He was checked in his transports by the churches ringing out the lustiest peals he had ever heard.

Running to the window, he opened it, and put out his head. No fog, no mist, no night; clear, bright, stirring, golden day.

"What's to-day?" cried Scrooge, calling downward to a boy in Sunday clothes, who perhaps had loitered in to look about him.

"*Eh?*"

"What's to-day, my fine fellow?"

"To-day! Why it's *Christmas day*."

"It's Christmas day! I haven't missed it. Hallo, my fine fellow!"

"Hallo!"

"Do you know the Poulterer's, in the next street but one, at the corner?"

"I should hope I did."

"An intelligent boy! A remarkable boy! Do you know whether they've sold the prize Turkey that was hanging there? Not the little prize Turkey — the big one?"

"What, the one as big as me?"

"What a delightful boy! It is a pleasure to talk to him. Yes, my buck!"

"It's hanging there now."

"Is it? Go and buy it."

"Walk-*er*!" exclaimed the boy.

"No, no, I am in earnest. Go and buy it, and tell 'em to bring it here, that I may give them the direction where to take it. Come back with the man, and I'll give you a shilling. Come back with him in less than five minutes, and I'll give you a half a crown!"

The boy was off like a shot.

"I'll send it to Bob Cratchit's! He sha'n't know who sends it. It's twice the size of Tiny Tim." The hand in which he wrote the address was not a steady one, but write it he did, somehow, and went down stairs to open the street door, ready for the coming of the poulterer's man.

It was a Turkey! He never could have stood upon his legs, that bird. He would have snapped 'em short off in a minute, like sticks of sealing-wax.

Scrooge dressed himself "all in his best," and at last got out into the streets. The people were by this time pouring forth, as he had seen them with the Ghost of Christmas Present; and, walking with his hands behind him, Scrooge regarded everyone with a delighted smile. He looked so irresistibly pleasant, in a word, that three or four good-humoured fellows said, "Good morning, sir! A merry Christmas to you!" And Scrooge said often afterwards, that of all the blithe sounds he had ever heard, those were the blithest in his ears.

(CONSORT REMAINS SEATED.)

Music
"London Waits" or *"Il Est Né" (One verse)*

A Merry Christmas Bob

ACTOR. He was early at the office the next morning. Oh, he was early there. If he could only be there first, and catch Bob Cratchit coming late! That was the thing he had set his heart upon.

And he did it. The clock struck nine. No Bob. A quarter past. No Bob. Bob was full eighteen minutes and a half behind his time. Scrooge sat with his door wide open, that he might see him come into the tank.

Bob's hat was off before he opened the door; his comforter too. He was on his stool in a jiffy; driving away with his pen, as if he were trying to overtake nine o'clock.

"Hallo!" growled Scrooge, in his accustomed voice, as near as he could feign it. "What do you mean by coming here at this time of day?"

"I am very sorry, sir. I *am* behind my time."

"You are? Yes, I think you are. Step this way if you please."

"It's only once a year, sir. It shall not be repeated. I was making rather merry yesterday, sir."

"No, I'll tell you what, my friend. I am not going to stand this sort of thing any longer. And therefore," Scrooge continued, leaping from his stool, and giving Bob such a dig in the waist-coat that he staggered back into the tank again, — "and therefore I am about to raise your salary!"

Bob trembled, and got a little nearer to the ruler.

"A merry Christmas, Bob!" said Scrooge, with an earnestness that could not be mistaken, as he clapped him on the back. "A merrier Christmas, Bob, my good fellow, than I have given you for many a year! I'll raise your salary, and endeavor to assist your struggling family, and we will discuss your affairs this very afternoon, over a Christmas bowl of smoking bishop, Bob! Make up the fires, and buy a second coal-scuttle before you dot another *i*, Bob Cratchit!"

Scrooge was better than his word. He did it all, and infinitely more; and to Tiny Tim, who did not die, he was a second father. He became as good a friend, as good a master, and as good a man as the good old city knew, or any other good old city, town, or borough in the good old world. Some people laughed to see the alteration in him; but his own heart laughed, and that was quite enough for him.

He had no further intercourse with Spirits, but lived in that respect upon the Total Abstinence Principle ever afterwards; and it was always said of him that he knew how to keep Christmas well, if any man alive possessed the knowledge. May that be truly said of us, and all of us!

(CONSORT STANDS to sing. ACTOR for "God Bless Us Every One!" moves to podium.

Music
"Christmas is a Comin' The Goose is Getting Fat!"

(CONSORT SITS AFTER SINGING.)

God Bless Us Every One

ACTOR. *(With great good humor, of joy—this crowning gift of the Cratchit's Christmas—the entrance of the pudding, this offering of the evening, "blazing...bedight with Christmas holly stuck into the top!" that crowns the gift of family, the grace of the season.)*

Hallo! A great deal of steam! The pudding was out of the copper. A smell like a washing-day! That was the cloth. A smell like an eating-house and a pastrycook's next door to each other, with a laundress's next door to that! That was the pudding! In half a minute Mrs. Cratchit entered — flushed, but smiling proudly —with the pudding, like a speckled cannon-ball, so hard and firm, blazing in half of half-a-quartern of ignited brandy, and bedight with Christmas holly stuck into the top.

Oh, a wonderful pudding! Bob Cratchit said, and calmly too, that he regarded it as the greatest success achieved by Mrs. Cratchit since their marriage. Mrs. Cratchit said that now the weight was off her mind, she would confess she had had her doubts about the quantity of flour. Everybody had something to say about it, but nobody said or thought it was at all a small pudding for a large family. It would have been flat heresy to do so. Any Cratchit would have blushed to hint at such a thing.

At last the dinner was all done, the cloth was cleared, the hearth swept, and the fire made up. The compound in the jug being tasted, and considered perfect, apples and oranges were put upon the table, and a shovel-full of chestnuts on the fire. Then all the Cratchit family drew round the hearth, in what Bob Cratchit called a circle, meaning half a one; and at Bob Cratchit's elbow stood the family display of glass. Two tumblers, and a custard-cup without a handle. These held the hot stuff from the jug, however, as well as golden goblets would have done; and Bob served it out with beaming looks, while the chestnuts on the fire sputtered and cracked noisily. Then Bob proposed:

"A Merry Christmas to us all, my dears. God bless us!"

Which all the family re-echoed.

"God bless us every one!" said Tiny Tim, the last of all.

(Piano, or organ, begins a light pattern of chords under the following reading of Luke. The reading ended, the ACTOR invites the audience to join THE CONSORT and the AC-TORS in the final carol. The chords will build as the invitation ends and becomes the introduction to the carol. CONSORT STANDS as the invitation to the audience to join is offered.)

Luke II Verses 10 - 14

ACTOR. (*This last, great gift—the good tidings of great joy, the star, the baby…*) And the angel said unto them, Fear not: for behold, I bring you good tidings of great joy, which shall be to all people. For unto you is born this day in the city of David a Saviour, which is Christ the Lord.

And this shall be a sign unto you; Ye shall find the babe wrapped in swaddling clothes, lying in a manger. And suddenly there was with the angel a multitude of the heavenly host praising God, and saying, "Glory to God in the highest and on earth peace, good will toward men."

(ACTOR invites audience to join in singing…)

Music
"We Wish You a Merry Christmas" or *"Joy to the World"*

(ALL Sing.)

(ACTORS and CONSORT join in wishing the audience a…)

Very Merry Christmas!

CURTAIN

PRODUCTION NOTES

Set

Actors. Podiums, stage left and right. Appropriate seats for the actors arranged behind or to the side of each podium.

Consort seated in an arc of chairs, stage center either upstage or downstage of the podiums, depending on the sight lines and the levels of the playing area.

This ground plan can be imposed, adapted for almost any venue — church, auditorium, theatres large and small. Obviously it should be adapted to suit the size of the company and the Consort, and can be altered to suit the size of the playing area and the audience.

Seasonal decoration, ornamentation is clearly desirable, but not essential. Flowers, poinsettias, wreaths, a tree, greens, lights — whatever is appropriate for the playing area. A Church setting does serves the production well.

See notes in the introduction, as well.

Lights

Basically there are three areas—each podium, left and right, and a center area for the Consort. If the areas can be controlled individually, that would be best, illuminating the actor or Consort when featured, dimming the areas not in use slightly.

Costumes

Treat the evening as a bright and beautiful Christmas party, festive clothing, perhaps tuxes for the men, simple colorful evening dresses for the women. But anything (almost) will do as long as the actors and singers are comfortable and a sense of occasion is created. I would avoid costumes, period coats and hats, etc.

Props

Scripts, music, for the actors and the Consort in uniformly colored binders — red or black, perhaps.

Most important, as in all productions whatever the play: Choices in performance and production should SERVE THE TEXT.

*Enchanting Plays and Musicals for Families
from the New York State Theatre Institute*

"A treat."—*Daily Gazette*
THE CANTERVILLE GHOST
A play with music adapted by John Vreeke *from the novel by* Oscar Wilde
Music and lyrics by Will Severin and George David Weiss

"Murder most entertaining."—*Metroland*
A KILLINGS TALE
An original mystery by W.A. Frankonis

"Those ten and older will find a lot of magic."—*NewsDay*
A LITTLE PRINCESS
Adapted by John Vreeke *from the story by* Frances Hodgson Burnett
Music and underscoring by Severin *and* George David Weiss

"Dazzling."—*Backstage*
A TALE OF CINDERELLA
Book by W.A. Frankonis /*Music by* Will Severin *and*
George David Weiss /*Lyrics by* George David Weiss

"A delight....Bustles ... with holiday good cheer."—*Metroland*
MIRACLE ON 34TH STREET
Comedy with music adapted by Will Severin, Patricia Di Benedetto
Snyder *and* John Vreeke *from the novel by* Valentine Davies
Music by Will Severin

"A crackling piece of theatre."—*Daily Gazette*
SHERLOCK'S SECRET LIFE
A play with music by Ed. Lange
Based on characters created by Sir Arthur Conan Doyle
Music and underscoring composed by Will Severin

"A delightful confection."—*Daily Gazette*
VASILISA THE FAIR (The Frog Princesses)
A play with music created by the New York State Theatre Institute